rfuge . . . no . . . t'

Gangsters! . . . that's it

raitors! . . . Woodlice! . . .

reckers! . . . Mountebanks!

Signed: Haddock.

For Jean-Baptiste
For Ivar Ch'Avar

The author would like to thank all those whose invaluable knowledge
and insights have helped him in the making of this book.
Special thanks to Michel Beirnaert, Biniou, Roger Caffiaux, Captain Antoine Champeaux,
Guillaume le Buanec, Philippe Lefever, Cyrille Mozgovine, Professor J. Vercruysse, Jean-Pierre Zeder.

First published in French in 1991 by Casterman
This edition first published in 2021 by Farshore

An imprint of HarperCollins*Publishers*
1 London Bridge Street, London SE1 9GF
www.farshore.co.uk

HarperCollins*Publishers*
1st Floor, Watermarque Building, Ringsend Road
Dublin 4, Ireland

Illustrations from The Adventures of Tintin © Hergé
© Casterman, 1991

Black-and-white illustrations on pages 18, 21, 27, 28, 29, 31, 32, 34, 35, 38, 40, 41, 44, 45, 46, 48, 49, 52,
53, 59, 60, 61, 62, 64, 66, 67, 69, 71, 73, 74, 76, 78, 80, 81, 82, 83, 85, 90, 92 and 93 © Shutterstock, 2021

With special thanks to Tom McBrien and Tim Jones

ISBN 978 00 0 849735 4
1
Printed in Estonia

Farshore takes its responsibility to the planet and its inhabitants very seriously.
We aim to use papers from well-managed forests run by responsible suppliers.

MIX
Paper from
responsible sources

FSC
www.fsc.org

FSC™ C007454

ALBERT ALGOUD

BLISTERING BARNACLES

An A-Z of the rants,
rambles and rages of
Captain Haddock

THE FINE ART
OF INSULT

Like the Greek hero Achilles, Captain Haddock owes his immortality to his tumultuous rages. It is his exuberant and irascible turn of phrase, more even than his illustrious exploits, that has seen him become one of the most popular heroes in the twentieth-century mythology that is The Adventures of Tintin.

Haddock is, of course, known for his alcoholic tendencies, however it is not rum or whisky, but words, that truly intoxicate our fiery friend. Powerless to resist his urges, Haddock glugs from an endless lexicon of dizzying insults, which he proceeds to shower upon his hapless enemies. Once a tirade takes hold, the Captain's tongue is unrestrained, and nothing short of verbal delirium can be expected.

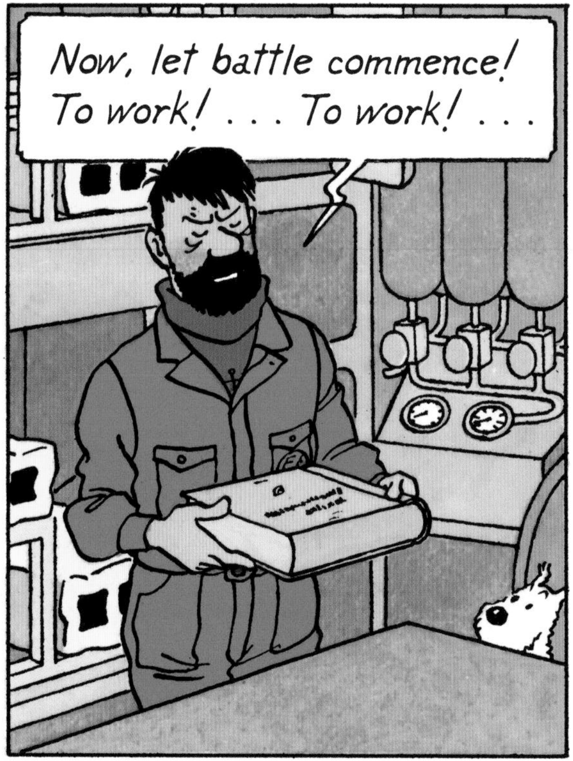
Now, let battle commence! To work! . . . To work! . . .

THE FINE ART OF INSULT

For a hero as singular as the Captain, only a truly original verbal repertoire will do. A standard, everyday insult may offer him some catharsis. But to bring an enemy to his knees, to harangue him to an early grave, something far more inventive is required. No swearwords, mind you. Barely a whiff of slang. We never hear vulgar expletives from Haddock's foaming mouth. His language is far from sordid and it is devoid of viciousness.

It is not only Haddock who vents using a vocabulary perfectly tailored to his temperament. A boundless passion for anathema is part of literary tradition. Think of all the fierce polemicists who have all wielded words as weapons in the war against wickedness and mediocrity. From Juvenal to Céline, Rabelais to Léon Bloy, Menippean satire to Dada and the Surrealists, writers have always used words to free themselves from anger and despair.

With access to an extraordinarily diverse panoply of insults, Haddock fights in a league of his own. He plucks branches from a bewildering array of thematic trees with which to fashion his devastating arrows. Anatomy, botany, chemistry, entomology, ethnology, history, literature, medicine, meteorology, ornithology, psychiatry, theology and zoology are just some of the topics exploited by the Captain's encyclopaedic rage.

THE FINE ART OF INSULT

Haddock also puts back into circulation, in delightfully unexpected ways, archaic or unusual terms, such as ectoplasm, abecedarian, anthropithecus, picaroon and mountebank. Convention flies out the window as these gems of vocabulary become illuminated in the glare of Haddock's fury, firing straight into the reader's imagination and engraving themselves upon their memory. Some phrases, such as 'blistering barnacles' and 'thundering typhoons', have become classics; others will continue to puzzle and intrigue the curious reader.

This book is not intended to serve as a museum, preserving Haddock's words in aspic. Rather, it celebrates a living lexicon. Haddock is a curator of language, an endlessly creative inventor. He plucks words from their humdrum everyday usage, and shoots them like arrows into the air, watching them fill with fresh sap and renewed vigour as they soar. He gives vocabulary back its resonance. He forges unexpected metaphors. He strikes down his enemies with round after round of blistering verbal imagery.

In classical poetry, 'inspiration' was described as a type of intoxication conferred by the gods. It is no coincidence that, in Hergé's work, the character chosen to embody such inspired verbal wizardry is the ever drunken Haddock.

THE FINE ART OF INSULT

The result of extensive research and revision, this dictionary is intended as both a lexicon, providing information on the meaning and use of each term, as well as a guidebook to the world inhabited by Captain Haddock. Included too are Haddockisms, the Captain's unique, original creations. Alongside the definitions, readers will recognise a rich selection of Hergé's comic strip artwork, illustrating the Captain in his full, incandescent glory.

It is my hope that, while enjoying this book, you too will find fitting words to deploy when insults of your own are required. May you, like the Captain, extend the limits of language and do justice to his fierce and fiery imagination.

ALBERT ALGOUD

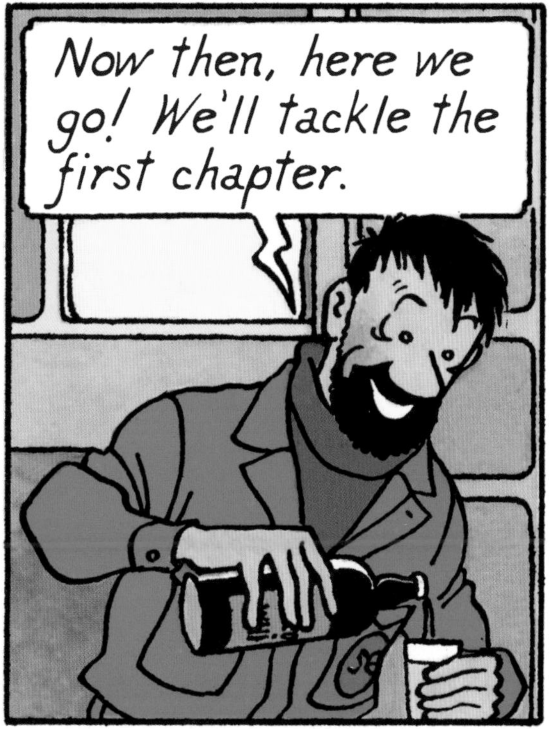
Now then, here we go! We'll tackle the first chapter.

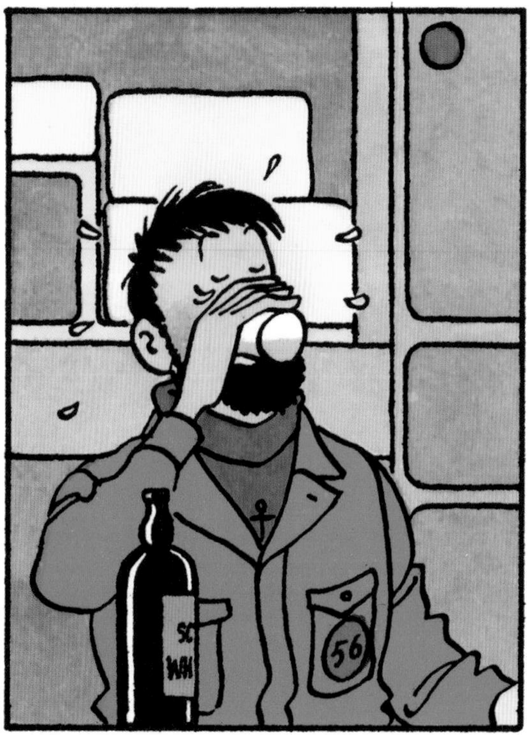
SC
WH
56

AARDVARK

An African mammal, with a long head, a tubular snout and pointed ears. Shy and nocturnal, aardvarks live in deep burrows and feed on ants and termites that they pick up with their very long, worm-like tongues. This is the first in a rich lexicon of unusual insults, which often bear little relation to the situation in hand but demonstate an exuberant delight in words and language.

Also: anamorphic aardvark

ABECEDARIAN

An abecedarian is defined as either an alphabetic sequence or something lacking in sophistication. It seems fair that Haddock means the latter, as it is addressed at what one must assume is full volume in the direction of a speeding car that has just attempted to run him over.

ABOMINABLE SNOWMAN

A legendary ape-like creature, also known as the Yeti, originating in Himalayan folklore and still believed by some to live in the Himalayan mountains in South and East Asia. Supposed evidence of the creature's existence includes photos, videos and casts taken of large footprints. The Abominable Snowman, as the creature has become known in the West, is now an icon of cryptozoology.

Also: you infernal impersonations of abominable snowmen

ABRACADABRA

A word said by conjurors when performing a magic trick or, more generally, denoting language used to give the impression of arcane knowledge or power. Though Haddock is largely a sceptic about matters supernatural, he becomes somewhat besotted with stage magic in *The Seven Crystal Balls*. Like many of his other crazes, however, this one is short-lived, due to a somewhat embarrassing and inadvertent stage incursion.

ALCOHOLIC

One suffering from alcoholism. This insult leaves one wondering if the Captain has much self-awareness; yet he does renounce alcohol on more than one occasion. It is possible, of

Come on, you old alcoholic, unless you're too scared!

course, that this particular affront may, in the past, have been levelled at Haddock himself, and that he is merely reflecting it back at others. In the case of the Yeti, whose continuing love of alcohol is somewhat Haddock's own fault, it does rather seem hypocritical.

Also: drunken old ape; old alcoholic

ANACHRONISM

An anachronism is something that more properly belongs to a period other than that in which it exists, thereby making it conspicuously old-fashioned or out-dated. As a retired sea captain, Haddock himself is something of an anachronism. Does the insult reflect his scepticism about his (admittedly very exciting) retirement?

ANACOLUTHON

An anacoluthon occurs when an expected grammatical sequence is interrupted or absent. An anacoluthia – the sudden switch from one syntactic structure to another – is a stylistic way to express an irrepressible emotion, but most of the time it is simply an error. The stupidity of other people is a constant irritation to Haddock, who hates any kind of inconsistency or lack of clarity, and is not slow to draw attention to it. From the political machinations of General Tapioca to his constant lack of patience with Thomson and Thompson, the Captain is not one to suffer fools gladly, or indeed with *politesse*.

ANTE-DILUVIAN BULLDOZER

Ante-diluvian refers to something belonging to the time before the biblical Flood as described in the chapter Genesis. Like anachronism, it is used by Haddock to rail against that which he considers to be absurdly and offensively out-dated.

ANTHROPITHECUS

A primate, the intermediary between monkey and early man.

Sir Francis Haddock, captain of *The Unicorn*, and lookalike ancestor of Captain Haddock, first used the term in 1698 to insult the pirate Red Rackham.

ANTHROPOID

Resembling a human being. A powerful insult, for the fact that it implies the person in question is somewhat less than human.

Also: gibbering anthropoids

ANTHROPOPHAGUS

A cannibal; an eater of human flesh. Haddock uses this arcane but exuberant term twice in the course of his adventures. The no-less-offensive,

but far more familar, 'cannibal', he uses eleven times in anger.

ARABESQUE

A position in ballet dancing or, in art, a design of flowing lines.

ARABIAN NIGHTMARE

The Thousand and One Nights, known also as *Arabian Nights*, is a collection of Middle Eastern folktales compiled in Arabic during the Islamic Golden Age. *Aladdin's Wonderful Lamp* and *Ali Baba and the Forty Thieves* are among the best known tales in the collection. This cleverly wrought insult is aimed at Haddock's mini nemesis, the mischievous Abdullah, who will surely be aware of its literary origins!

ARTICHOKE

Eaten as a vegetable, the artichoke is a round, thistle-like plant with thick, edible leaves arranged around a flower head or 'heart'.

ASSASSIN

Someone who kills a famous or important person, usually for political reasons.

AUTOCRAT

A ruler with unlimited power who demands complete obedience from their subjects. Marshal Plekszy Gladz and General Tapioca are autocrats. In 1932, long before meeting Tintin, Haddock penned a book called, in French, *On a volé un Dictateur*, published by Gallimard, which testifies to his hatred of autocrats. Haddock's career as an author was short-lived.

AZTEC

An ancient civilisation from Mexico who dominated the country and established a great empire, centred on the valley of Mexico, until the Spanish conquest of the sixteenth century.

B

Baboon! Freshwater swab!

Hello, my old friend!

BABOON

An African catarrhine monkey. Baboons have greyish-brown or olive-coloured fur and patches of rough, protruding skin on their buttocks, known as 'ischial callosities', that allow them to sleep sitting upright on thin branches, beyond the reach of predators. These callosities are often brightly coloured. Baboons have long canine teeth and their elongated muzzle resembles that of a dog. They live in groups of around 50 individuals, known as a 'troop'.

Also: macrocephalic baboon

BABY-SNATCHER

A person who steals a baby from its pram; a cradle-snatcher. A truly heinous crime and a weighty insult.

Also: body-snatcher

BAGPIPER

One who plays the bagpipes, a musical instrument consisting of a leather bag and two or three pipes with holes that emit shrill and penetrating sounds.

Bandit! . . . Bootlegger! . . . Bashi-bazouk! . . . Breathalyser! Brigand!

Keep your hair on, Captain . . . I mean . . . Come and let me try to get that hat off!

BALD-HEADED BUDGERIGAR

A small, long-tailed parrot, known for its friendly, chatty disposition. Quite how friendly Haddock's bald-headed version is, is anyone's guess.

BANDICOOT

Small, nocturnal marsupials native to Australia and New Guinea. They have V-shaped faces and prominent noses, and make their nests in shallow holes in the ground. The name 'bandicoot' is an Anglicised version of the word 'pandi-kokku', meaning 'pig-rat', in the Telugu language of South India.

Also: lily-livered bandicoots

BANDIT

A robber, typically belong to an armed gang.

Also: Baltic bandit.

BASHI-BAZOUK

A bashi-bazouk was a mercenary soldier in the Ottoman army. Recruited by the sultans to boost the regular army, the bashi-bazouks did not receive pay or wear a uniform, but lived off loot seized from civilian populations. They formed a formidable, undisciplined cavalry with a reputation for brutal violence.

During the Crimean War in the nineteenth century, their number reached 40,000. During the Balkan Wars of 1876–1878, they carried out the bloody suppression of the Bulgarian population and the surrounding area, hence the vicious Haddockism 'Carpathian bashi-bazouks'.

BATH-TUB ADMIRAL

In the Captain's vivid imagination, a bath tub becomes a boat of sorts – a boat ill-equipped for ocean crossings and commanded by an admiral of limited abilities.

BEAST

A brutal or uncivilised person; a wild animal, especially a large quadruped.

BEELZEBUB

A god of the Philistines, as mentioned in the biblical Old Testament; Satan or any devil or demon.

BEETLE

Insects of the order Coleoptera with crushing mouthparts and folding wings protected by a pair of horny cases, or 'elytra'. The Captain has always had an uneasy relationship with insects; they always seem to provoke his ire. From exterminating mosquitos en masse in *The Calculus Affair*, to being stung on his nose by a bee in *The Castafiore Emerald*, Haddock has little regard for matters entomic.

Also: Balkan beetle; black beetle

BELEMNITE

Belemnites were marine animals with squid-like bodies and a hard internal skeletons that lived during the Jurassic and Cretaceous periods. They became extinct at about the same time as the dinosaurs and our knowledge of them comes from fossil records.

BIG-HEAD

A conceited or arrogant person.

BIRD OF ILL OMEN

A person who brings bad news.

BLACK MARKETEER

Someone who sells goods on the black market. Haddock has a healthy contempt for dodgy dealing.

BLACKGUARD

An contemptible person without principles; a scoundrel.

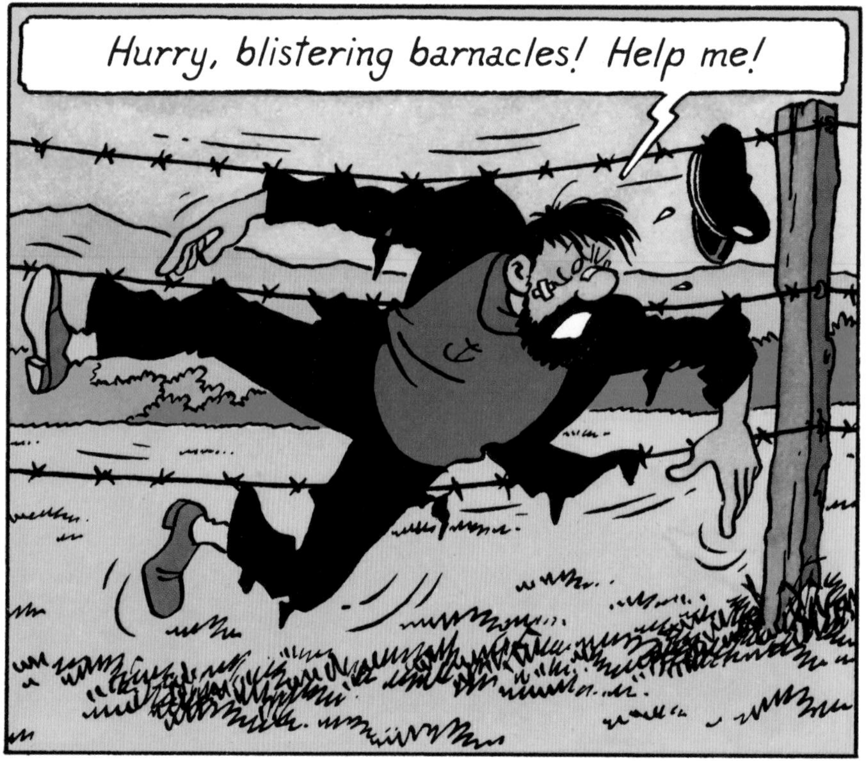
Hurry, blistering barnacles! Help me!

BLISTERING BARNACLES

A barnacle is a type of non-mobile arthropod that clings to the bottom of marine vessels. One of Haddock's masterpieces of alliterative abuse, the 'blue blistering barnacle' seems to be entirely a product of his own mind, with a nautical nod to his former life. It is interesting to note that other sailors of his acquaintance are also fond of alliterative curses; when his old friend, Captain Chester, comes across Haddock again, he is in the middle of addressing him as a 'seismic semaphore' for knocking his pipe out of his mouth. Only Haddock, however, could raise the humble barnacle to the pinnacle of imprecation. The phrase is so characteristic of Haddock that the young Abdullah turns it into his nickname.

Also: billions of bilious blue blistering barnacles;
billions of bilious blue blistering barbecued barnacles;
billions of blue blistering boiled and barbecued barnacles;
blue blistering barnacles in a thundering typhoon;
billions of bilious blue blistering barnacles in a thundering typhoon;
blistering Yetis, it's the Barnacle;
yettering barnacles, it's the blister

BLITHERING BOMBARDIER

A bombardier is the member of a bomber aircrew responsible for aiming and releasing the bombs.

BLUE BLISTERING BELLBOTTOMED BALDERDASH

Balderdash is talk that is senseless or stupid.

BLOODSUCKER

Confronted with the hostile fauna of a virgin forest, Haddock bellows this invective at both the alligator he has just escaped and the mosquitos that continue to harass him.

BLUNDERBUSS

A short musket with large bore and flared muzzle, used to scatter shot at short range; a clumsy person.

BODY-SNATCHER

A person who robbed graves and sold the corpses for dissection, during the eighteenth and nineteenth centuries. The only bodies legally available to medical students for the study of anatomy were the remains of executed criminals. The demand for corpses exceeded the supply and criminal gangs were quick to spot morbid opportunity.

Also: baby-snatcher

BONE-HEAD

A stupid or obstinate person.

BOOTLEGGER

A person who makes, smuggles, or sells something made illicitly. The term 'bootlegging' originated in the US Midwest in the 1880s, where restrictions on the manufacture and sale of liquor drove smugglers to conceal flasks of illicit liquor in their boot tops. The term spread more widely under Prohibition, which began in 1920 and lasted until 1933, during which the production, importation, transportation and sale of all alcoholic beverages were banned nationwide. Criminal gangs moved in to take control of the supply of liquor in many cities.

BORGIA

A member of the Borgia family, whose name has become synonymous with ruthless political ambition and treachery. Originally from Valencia, Spain, this influential noble family settled in Italy and became powerful in ecclesiastical and political circles in the 1400s and 1500s. Cesare Borgia famously attempted to establish his own principality in central Italy, while his sister Lucrezia became one of the most powerful women in the court of Italy.

BOTTLED BILGE-WATER

Dirty water that collects inside the bilges on a ship.

BOUGAINVILLEA

A climbing plant with red or purple flowers, commonly found in hot climates. This is an odd term for Haddock to use, as it is Professor Calculus who is green-fingered, and this variety seems more suited to the Professor's gift for cultivation. Haddock's love of nature is more rustic; life at Marlinspike involves country walks, rather than greenhouses.

BRAGGARD

A boastful person or bragger.

Also: scoffing braggard

BRAT

An ill-mannered, unruly or annoying child. Haddock refers to his young nemesis Abdullah in this way.

BREATHALYSER

A device for estimating the amount of alcohol in the breath. One of Haddock's most obscure insults.

BRIGAND

Originally a brigand was a soldier who travelled on foot. The term has come to mean someone who attacks and robs others, especially in mountains or forests.

BRONTOSAURUS

A sauropod dinosaur, common in North America during Jurassic times, and nowadays known as apatosaurus. These huge creatures measured up to 22 metres in length, weighing up to 30 tonnes. A 'brontosaurus' skeleton can be admired at the Natural History Museum in Klow, capital of Syldavia.

BRUTE

A person with brutal and uncivilised tendencies; an animal that is not a human.

Also: loathsome brute

BUCCANEER

Pirates who preyed on Spanish ships in America and the Caribbean in the seventeenth and eighteenth centuries. They were also known as the 'Brethren of the Coast' for their history of joining forces to plunder the ships and coasts of the Spanish colonies. The French buccaneers from Turtle Island and the English buccaneers from Jamaica occasionally set sail together as allies, with the French buccaneers from the island of Santo Domingo joining as auxiliaries. Much of Haddock's repertoire is nautical in nature, with a preference for the seamier side of the high seas, perhaps as a result of his genetic inheritance from Sir Francis Haddock, the man who defeated the great pirate Red Rackham. Sworn enemies of the honest sailor since time immemorial, the buccaneer, pirate or filibuster represented the worst of human nature at sea – hence Haddock's special dislike of them.

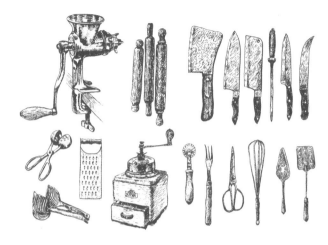

BULLY

A champion of the oppressed, Haddock cannot abide a bully, with a particular disdain for those who lack respect for other human beings. His verbal assault of the slave trader in *The Red Sea Sharks* shows his fearlessness in confronting injustice.

BUTCHER

A shopkeeper who cuts up and sells meat; a brutal and indiscriminate murderer.

CACHINNATING COCKATOO

If you were anywhere near a cachinnating cockatoo, you would certainly know it. Cachination is laughing, guffawing or cackling so loudly that tears roll down your cheeks.

CANNIBAL

Someone who eats human flesh. In using humankind's oldest taboo as an expletive, Haddock is merely continuing an age-old disgust with the barbaric practice of eating one's own species.

CARPATHIAN

A person who comes from the Carpathian mountain range of central and eastern Europe, a chain that extends from Slovakia to Romania, and which includes the country of Syldavia, the base from which Calculus's moon-rocket is launched.

Also: Carpathian bashi-bazouks; Carpathian caterpillar

CARPET-SELLER

A merchant or businessperson who is prepared to sell anything for a healthy profit.

CATERPILLAR

The wormlike larva of a butterfly or moth. It has a segmented body, three pairs of true legs on the thorax, several pairs of prolegs on the abdomen and very strong jaws.

Also: Carpathian caterpillar

CENTIPEDE

Despite its name, this long, thin arthropod may have anything from 30 to 354 legs. Many centipedes have a venomous bite to subdue prey.

Also: stubborn South American centipedes

CERCOPITHECUS

Cercopithecidae are the largest primate family, numbering 138 species. Baboons and macaques are all *cercopithecidae*.

CHUMP CHOP

A chump chop is a cut of meat, usually from a lamb, consisting of the trimmed cut of the boneless part of the leg. It can then be cooked or roasted. Haddock uses this to describe two villains that he has just restrained, before giving them a verbal roasting.

CLEVER DICK

Someone who is excessively opinionated or self-satisfied; a know-all.

CLUMSY FOOTED QUADRUPED

An animal with four legs, somewhat unsteady on its feet. An insult Haddock levels with vehemence at his Andean nemeses, the llamas.

Also: cushion-footed quadrupeds

COELACANTH

This nocturnal fish was believed to have become extinct 65 million years ago. However, two species of this four-legged 'fossil fish' were found alive and well, one off the coast of Africa in 1938, and the others in Indonesian waters in the late 1990s.

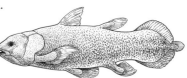

COLEOPTERA

With more than 350,000 described species of beetle, this is the largest order, or group, of animals on Earth. The order contains about 40 per cent of all the known insect species on the planet.

COLOCYNTH

Also known as bitter apple, desert gourd and vine of Sodom, the desert plant *Citrullus colocynthis* is native to the Mediterranean and Asia. Its ripe fruit and seeds can be pulped to make a medical laxative.

CONFOUNDED RATTLETRAP

Haddock makes frequent use of the adjective 'confounded', meaning bewildered or damned, one of a string of expletives addressed at the engine-room telegraph in *The Red Sea Sharks*, broken at a moment of extreme jeopardy. Haddock curses animate and inanimate objects with equal vehemence.

Also: confounded jukebox

CORSAIR

A fast ship sailed by a government-sanctioned crew to pursue and board enemy merchant vessels. Although privateers are not to be confused with pirates, with this invective Captain Haddock stresses the difference between seamen who, like him, instinctively obey the code of honour of the profession and sailors of fortune.

COWARD

A person who is lacking in courage, easily frightened and tries to avoid any danger or difficulty to the extent of hiding or running away. The tradition of the captain 'going down with the ship' bears witness to the extent to which cowardice is frowned upon in maritime circles. Haddock is no exception, and, though we never get the chance to see how he would deal with this particular scenario, his bravery is evident throughout his adventures. In *Tintin in Tibet,* he shows that he is prepared to sacrifice his life to avoid pulling his friend from the mountain.

CRAB APPLE

The small, sour applelike fruit of a tree that bears the same name. The fruit of some varieties is used to make jellies and jams. Possibly chosen by the Captain for its association with the ocean-dwelling crustacean, the fruit of *Malus sylvestris*, the crab apple, has no connection with crabs. It is suggested that the tree's gnarly bark may have given the tree its name; Haddock is equally rugged in appearance, at least when at sea.

CRO-MAGNON

The name given to fossils of a type of prehistoric human first discovered in 1868 in a cave at Cro-Magnon near the town of Les Eyzies-de-Tayac in the Dordogne region of France. These early modern humans lived across Europe during Late Paleolithic times, and used sophisticated tools of Aurignacian culture.

CROOK

The word describes a shepherd's staff with its curved hook. The bend of this instrument gives rise to the idea of something that is 'bent' or 'crooked', which describes a dishonest person, a criminal or a cheat.

CRY-BABY

Someone who sheds tears easily and frequently. It is mostly used as a derogatory term to describe someone who is quick to cry and can be made to weep harder if they are called 'a cry-baby'.

CUT-THROAT

A murderer or other violent criminal. Someone who uses ruthless, backstabbing methods to get what they want.

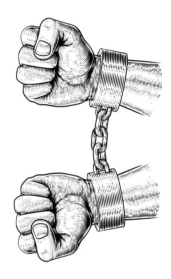

CYCLONE

The 'cyclone' or 'cyclonic separator' is a rotating device that uses centrifugal force to remove solids from a gas, first patented in 1885 by the American John M. Finch. More commonly, a cyclone refers to a violent storm that spins like a whirlpool. The Captain, having sailed the tropical seas where cyclones form, speaks from experience when he uses this image.

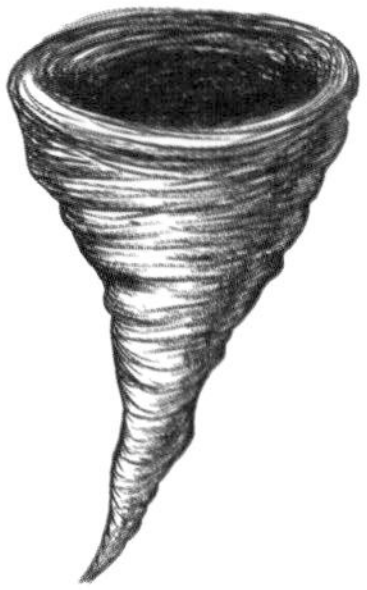

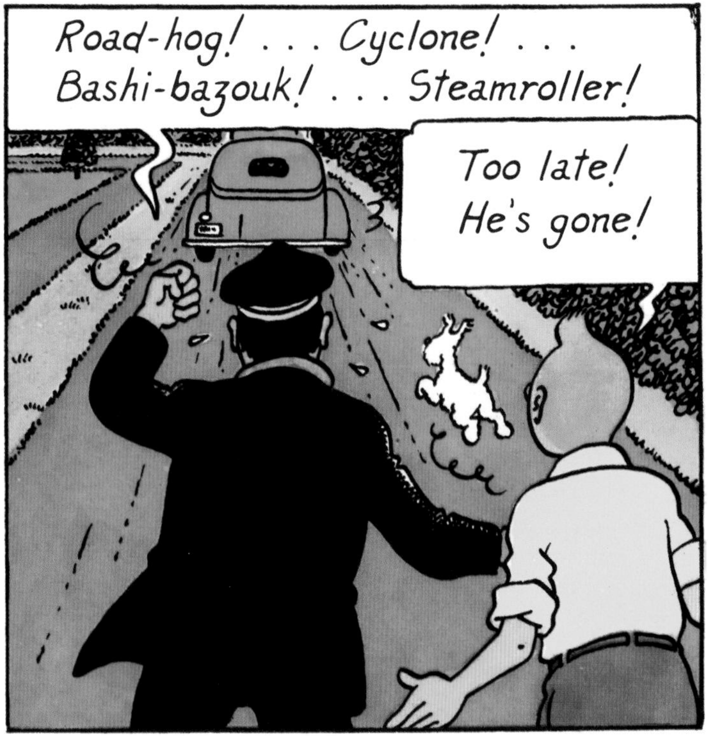
Road-hog! . . . Cyclone! . . . Bashi-bazouk! . . . Steamroller!
Too late! He's gone!

CYCLOTRON

The cyclotron is a type of particle accelerator, invented in the early 1930s by American physicists Ernest Orlando Lawrence and M. Stanley Livingston. A cyclotron uses electromagnetic fields to propel charged particles to very high speeds and energies. The device is still in widespread use today, with over 1500 cyclotron facilities in operation across 95 countries. The radioisotopes produced in a cyclotron are used to make medical drugs called radiopharmaceuticals, which in turn are used in the diagnosis and treatment of cancer.

D

DICTATORIAL DUCKBILLED DIPLODOCUS

An autocratic ruler with absolute power is dictatorial, liking to give orders and brooking no arguments with the right to control the lives of those around them. In *Tintin and the Picaros*, it seems that Haddock has finally met a demagogue that is his match: the verbose firebrand dictator General Tapioca. The spectacle of the Captain's rage boiling over as he watches Tapioca denounce him on television reaches its height when Haddock, millimetres from the screen, delivers the almighty and matchless insult: 'Nobody's more treacherous than you, you guano-gatherer!'

Also: diplodocus

DINOSAUR

Any of a group of land reptiles that became extinct at the end of the Cretaceous period 65 million years ago. They included some of the largest animal species that have lived on Earth. The name derives from the Greek *deinos*, meaning 'terrible' and *sauros*, meaning 'lizard'. Today's birds evolved from the dinosaurs. Also a person or thing that has become obsolete because it is not up-to-date.

DIPLODOCUS

A huge herbivorous dinosaur of the late Jurassic period. With its very long neck and tail, it measured 27 metres in length and weighed up to 20 tonnes.

Also: certified diplodocus, dictatorial duckbilled diplodocus

DIPSOMANIAC

Someone who gets drunk often and to excess; an alcoholic.

DIZZARD

A silly, foolish person or blockhead.

DOG

A quadruped hound of the genus *Canis*, which includes animals that are wild, kept as pets or trained for work. If someone is called a dog, the person describing them is being disapproving or offensive. Also a male dog, wolf or fox.

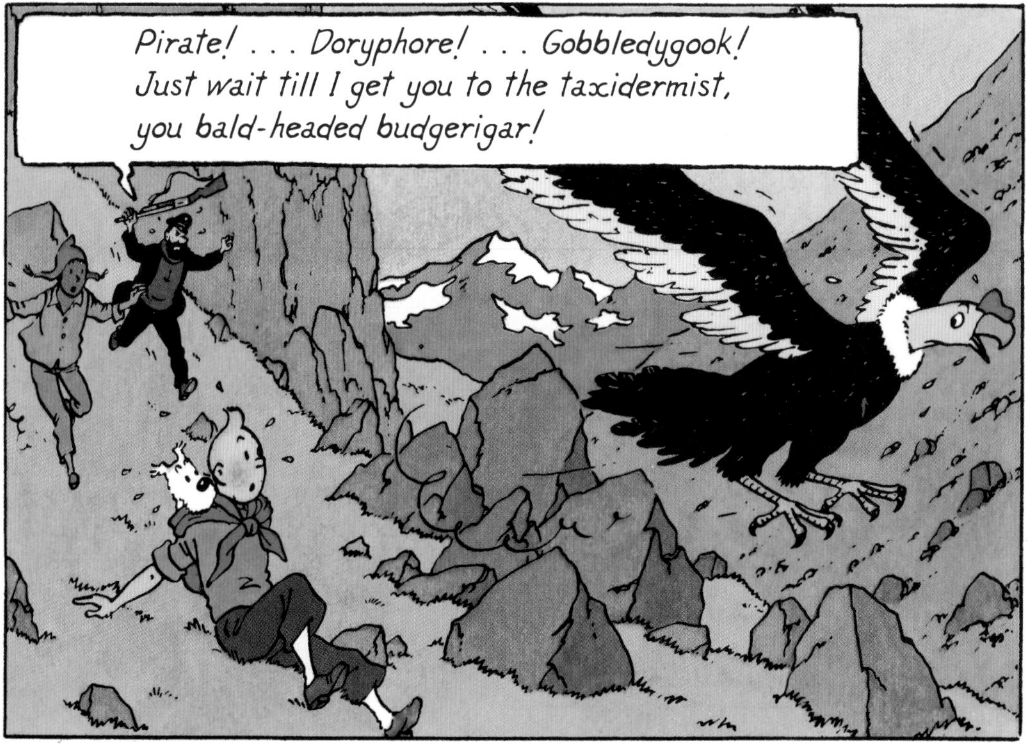
Pirate! . . . Doryphore! . . . Gobbledygook! Just wait till I get you to the taxidermist, you bald-headed budgerigar!

DONKEY

A famously stubborn, domesticated member of the horse family with short legs and long ears. Donkeys are descended from the African wild ass and are kept to be ridden or to carry heavy loads. Also a stupid or stubborn person.

DORYPHORE

A pedantic person who is an annoyingly persistent critic, complaining about minor mistakes.

DRATTED ANIMAL

Dratted means wretched or annoying. Haddock's relationships with animals is neatly summed up when speaking of Peru in *Prisoners of the Sun*: 'Blistering Barnacles, what a country. Is there no end to this mountainous menagerie?' They exist to pester and annoy him, to split in his face, to spoil his peace and quiet, to drink whatever he has his eye on, and to generally bring him grief. Not for him the close relationship that Tintin enjoys with Snowy – Haddock is not of an animal-loving nature.

DUCK-BILLED PLATYPUS

A small aquatic mammal from the monotreme order, native to Australia and New Guinea. The duck-billed platypus is renowned for its strange combination of uniquely adaptive features: a ducklike beak, webbed legs, a beaverlike tail and – in the case of males – venomous hooks on its hind legs. The female is oviparous and feeds her young by oozing milk from her skin.

DUNDER-HEADED ETHELRED

Ethelred II was only about twelve years old when he came to the throne of England in 978CE, after the murder of his half-brother. He is remembered as 'the Unready'. This probably originated from a pun on his name – Ethelred means 'noble-counsel' while the noun 'unraed' means 'an ill-considered plan'. This morphed into Ethelred No-counsel and from there to Ethelred the Unready, because he did little to prevent raids by the Danes during his reign, handing over Dane-geld in failed attempts to keep the raiders from England's shores.

DYNAMITER

An explosives expert who practises the handling and blasting of dynamite, an invention patented by Alfred Nobel in 1867.

ECTOPLASM

In parapsychology, ectoplasm is a viscous substance that may be produced by a medium, the intermediary between the human and spirit worlds, during a trance. During the nineteenth and early twentieth centuries, séances became a popular pastime – a thrilling encounter with the ghostly realm. Mediums claimed to be able to contact and communicate with spirits, which would often be those of deceased relatives or friends. Via the medium, loved ones would pose questions and receive answers, sometimes delivered in voices eerily mimicking those of the departed. The appearance of ectoplasm was a way for mediums to provide 'evidence' of the existence of these spirits and their capacity to physically manifest in the world of the living. Ectoplasm would seem to ooze from the body of the medium, for example from the mouth or ear. Sometimes it would coalesce into the face of the spirit who was supposedly talking. Early photography seemed to support these claims. Of course, in reality, these phenomena were carefully staged trickery, the medium spitting up cloth or paper they had previously swallowed. Other mediums cut out pictures from newspapers which they displayed once the lights went out. Conveniently, ectoplasm was known to only manifest under cover of darkness. The Captain, needless to say, is sceptical of all things pertaining to the spirit world.

Also: ectoplasmic byproduct

EGOIST

A selfish, conceited or self-centred person.

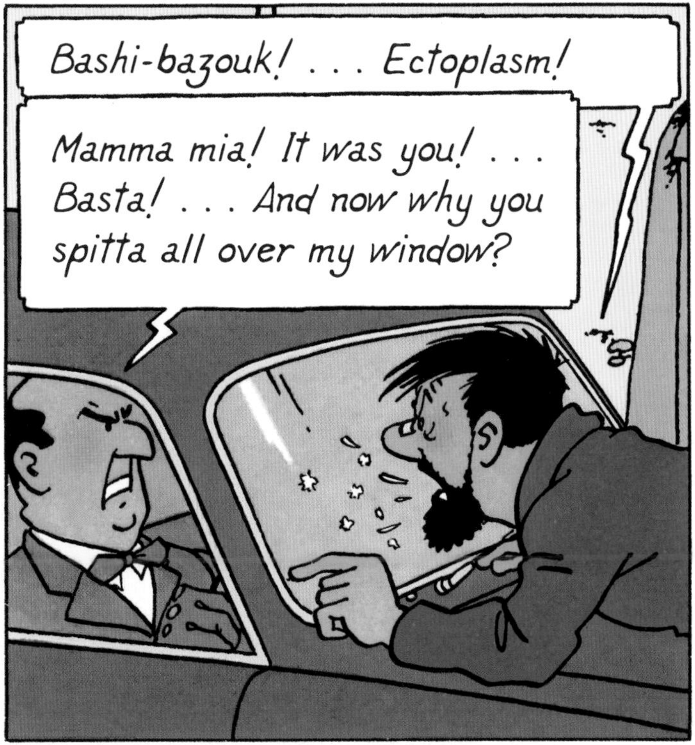
Bashi-bazouk! . . . Ectoplasm!
Mamma mia! It was you! . . . Basta! . . . And now why you spitta all over my window?

F

FANCY-DRESS FASCIST

A member of a mass movement of far-right authoritarian political ideology that dominated much of Europe from 1919 to 1945, although other countries also became totalitarian one-party states. Adolf Hitler in Germany, Benito Mussolini in Italy and Juan Perón in Argentina were prominent fascist leaders in the twentieth century. Haddock maintains a healthy contempt for the inauthentic, to go with his contempt for pomp and hypocrisy. It is somewhat ironic that when Tintin and Haddock defeat the arch 'fancy-dress fascist', General Tapioca, they are disguised as carnival clowns.

Also: fancy-dress freebooter

FAT FACE

An abusive term for someone with an unusually large face.

FAT-HEADED FIRE-RAISERS

A person who intentionally starts a fire in order to damage or destroy something, usually a building; an arsonist.

Blue blistering barnacles! . . . A lighted cigarette! The fat-headed fire-raisers!

FIDDLE DEE DEE

An exclamation of impatience, disbelief or scorn, equivalent to 'nonsense!'

FIDDLE-FADDLE

A dismissive and contemptuous description of trifling talk or action.

FIEND

A person who is extremely wicked, cruel or brutal; an evil spirit.

> Wreckers! ... Pirates! ...
> Filibusters! ... Picaroons!
> Leaving us in the lurch on a
> doomed ship! To Davy Jones
> with the lot of you!

FILIBUSTER

An archaic term for a pirate or buccaneer, deriving from the sixteenth-century Spanish *filibustero*.

FLAMING
JACK-IN-A-BOX

Originally used to describe a cheating swindler in the sixteenth century, Jack-in-a-box describes someone who pops up when you are least expecting it and usually when you don't want to see them. It is also a child's toy box that, when the lid is raised, releases the Jack, or puppet, on a spring to leap out and give delighted children a surprise.

FLYING SAUCER

A disc-shaped object in the sky that is believed to be an alien spacecraft; a UFO.

FOOL

A professional jester or clown employed in a royal or noble household to entertain people by telling jokes, singing songs and generally 'playing the fool', which is to say, acting in a silly way to get laughs. Also a person who acts unwisely; a person who is easily duped.

Also: clumsy fool

FOUR-LEGGED CYRANO

Before his nose was immortalised in the 1897 play by Edmond Rostand, Cyrano de Bergerac was an important French literary figure. As a young man, he served in the company of guards. After being seriously wounded at the Siege of Arras in 1640, he left the military and settled in Paris, where he studied under the philosopher and mathematician Pierre Gassendi. Here he wrote his most famous work, *A Voyage to the Moon*, a classic of early science fiction that satirises religious and astronomical beliefs of the time. Rostand's famous play is liberal in its interpretation of history. The cause of Cyrano's death, which according to Rostard, results from a head injury sustained when he was struck by a falling beam in the house of his patron, is disputed by academics.

FRAUD

A person or thing intended to deceive others; a trickster.

FRESHWATER SWAB

A life spent at sea has given our hero a distaste for those with more mundane existences, especially those who navigate fresh water, rather than the high seas. Haddock is most at home at sea and his contempt for those who find maritime life difficult is obvious. 'Freshwater sailor' or 'swab' is therefore the worst insult one could possibly address to a sailor.

Also: freshwater astronaut; freshwater pirate; freshwater politician; freshwater spaceman

GALLOWS BIRD

A person who deserves to be hanged. A gallows was the instrument used for the hanging.

Also: gallows fodder

GANG OF THIEVES

A group of people who work together in an organised fashion to steal things.

GANGSTER

A member of a violent criminal gang, one who would not think twice about taking a life in pursuit of a lucrative end.

GAS BAG

A windbag; a bag for holding gas such as a balloon or dirigible. Also a person who boasts, or who talks excessively about trivial matters.

Also: overdressed windbag

GIBBERING GHOST

Someone who talks very fast and in a confusing way is described as gibbering, often because they are afraid.

GIBBON

A small, slender ape of the family *Hylobatidae* that lives in the forests of southeast Asia. There are around 20 species of gibbon and they all have very long, powerful arms, no tail and a distinctive loud, hooting call.

GOAT

A stupid person, a fool. One of Haddock's more ill-advised epithets, in that it causes Professor Calculus great upset. In fact, Haddock calls Calculus a goat on numerous occasions, almost as a term of endearment, with only Calculus's deafness preventing him from hearing. When he finally does hear, however, in an episode of rage that takes place over several pages, the result is spectacular.

Also: acting the goat; interplanetary goat

GOBBLEDEGOOK

Gobbledegook is language that is hard to understand because it meanders and is so full of jargon that it makes no sense.

GOGGLER

Someone who stares, or goggles, at something with eyes wide open, especially if surprised or shocked.

GOOSECAP

A foolish or silly person.

GRAND PANJANDRUM

A self-important official or person of rank, derived from the eponymous hero of Samuel Foote's children's book *The Great Panjandrum Himself*.

GRAND PIANO

A large piano whose strings are set horizontally to the ground, often used for concerts or recordings.

GREAT FLAT-FOOTED GRIZZLY BEAR

The back of the adult brown bear, *Ursus arctos horribilis*, of North America is streaked with grey which gives it a grizzled appearance. Grizzly bears are large and ferocious carnivores.

GUANO-GATHERER

The effluvia of the ubiquitous seagull, guano is naturally familiar to Haddock. Tintin, in *Prisoners of the Sun*, is unaware of the term and the fortuitous arrival of a gull to drop its foul by-product on Thomson's hat spares Haddock the bother of making a vulgar explanation. Those who gather guano or, one presumes, any kind of excrement, are naturally contemptible in Haddock's eyes.

GUTTERSNIPE

A young hoodlum or street urchin; a gatherer of rubbish.

GYROSCOPE

A device consisting of a rotating disc mounted in a set of rings. The disc maintains its original direction of rotation regardless of the direction in which the rings are spinning.

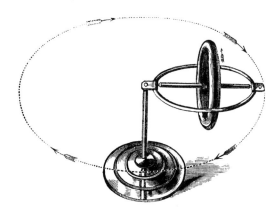

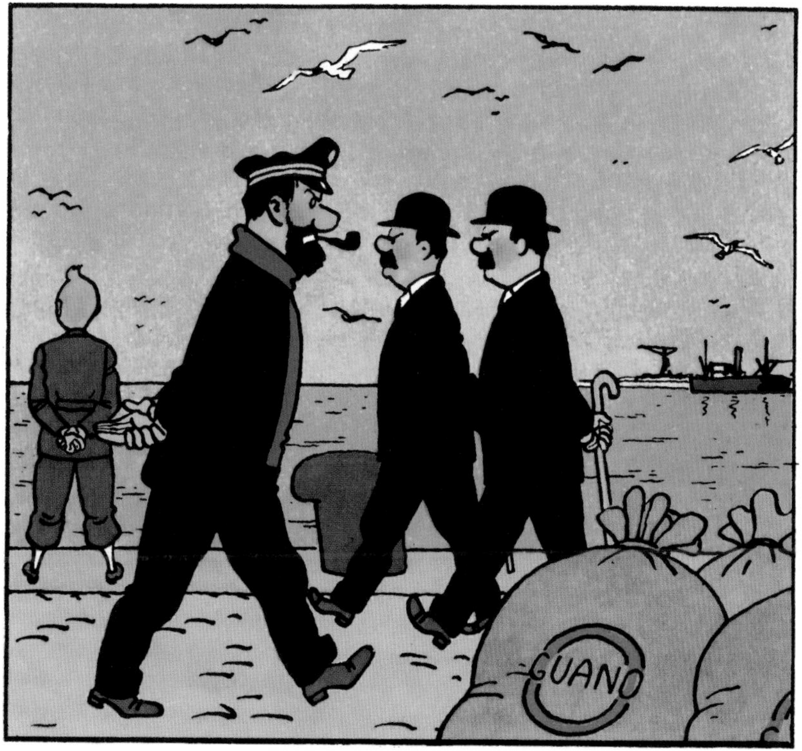
GUANO

HALF-BAKED HADDOCK

The Captain takes his now-iconic name from an edible sea fish found in the north Atlantic. This ironical self-insult – 'What sort of village idiot d'you take me for? Half-baked haddock?' – evokes a most unpleasant dish.

HARLEQUIN

A comic character originating in the Italian *commedia dell'arte*, Harlequin wears a suit patterned with coloured diamond shapes and a black mask, and carries a stick. In the English harlequinade he is the lover of Columbine. For Haddock, Harlequin is a ridiculous character, akin to a jester.

HERETIC

A heretic is a person whose opinions differ fundamentally from those of the Church, and who refuses to recognise its authority. A heretic is not to be confused with a heterodox, whose opinions diverge from official, established or orthodox beliefs, or a schismatic, who causes or promotes schism. A heretic is necessarily a heterodox, but a heterodox is not necessarily a heretic. A heretic is not necessarily a schismatic and a schismatic is not necessarily heretical. In relation to the Roman Catholic Church, the Greek Orthodox Church is schismatic; Protestants are schismatic *and* heretical, with only Catholics representing orthodoxy.

HIGHWAYMAN

These robbers thrived in England in the seventeenth and eighteenth centuries. Legend has it that a mounted highwayman dressed well, with a kerchief over his face, and used threats rather than violence, holding up coaches and carriages with the greetings 'Stand and deliver' and 'Your money or your life'. In reality, many highwaymen were not so well-mannered and robbed travellers brutally.

HIJACKER

People who use violence or threats to illegally take control of a vehicle, such as a lorry or plane, to force it to travel to a different place. The hijackers may have political motives, demanding something from a government. Also, people who steal from a vehicle after forcing it to stop.

HOCUS POCUS

Describes trickery or deceptive magical practices using mysterious incantations. Broadly a sceptic of the unexplained, Haddock's first response to the supernatural is to deny it. Faced with the possibility of genuine extra-terrestrials, his first response is 'So now we've come to flying saucers . . . we aren't as gullible as that!' Sailors on the whole are a superstitious lot, but not Haddock. When told that bad luck comes to those who pass on the wrong side of a chorten in *Tintin in Tibet*, his first response is incredulity. Naturally he complies so as not to offend the sensibilities of his companions, but makes his disdain clear.

HOLY HURRICANE

Hurricanes are the most extreme weather in Earth's atmosphere. They are giant circular storms that roll in from the east across the oceans, doing untold damage with ferocious winds and torrential rain when they hit land.

HOODLUM

A violent thug, gangster or rowdy street ruffian, particularly one that belongs to a gang.

HOOLIGAN

A young troublemaker, probably belonging to a gang, who likes to fight or cause damage in public places.

HUMAN FLOTSAM

People who are not wanted or considered to be important or useful.

HUMBUG

Dishonest, insincere rubbish spoken by someone that may be intended to deceive.

HYDROCARBON

A chemical compound containing only hydrogen and carbon, such as benzene or methane. Hydrocarbons are found in petrol, coal and natural gas.

ICONOCLAST

A follower of the eighteenth-century doctrine banning the use of imagery in religion. Iconoclasm was a doctrine that, while recognising the legitimacy of the cult of Christ, the Virgin Mary and the saints, prohibited the representation and veneration of their images. For a comic-book hero such as Haddock, who owes his fame to Hergé's pictures and the devotion they inspire, there is, of course, no more dangerous enemy than an iconoclast!

IDIOT

Someone who is very stupid. It can also be used to describe someone who is a fool or a clown.

Stand back, anachronisms! . . . Keep off, you imitation Incas, you!

IGNORAMUS

This somewhat outdated term describes an extremely ignorant person who does not have the knowledge you may think they should have.

Also: certified ignoramus

IMITATION INCA

The Incas originated in the Peruvian highlands in the twelth century and, at its height, their empire covered a large area of western South America, including territory in Peru, Equador, Bolivia, Argentina, Chile and Columbia. The Incan empire experienced an era of astonishing splendour before its destruction by the Spanish conquistadors. Coming across an Incan civilisation many years after they were supposed to have died out, Haddock's mind naturally turns to the ersatz. His rage and confusion causes him to let rip at the guards of the Temple of the Sun, who, as 'imitations', he considers to be devaluing the prestige and sacred history of the Incan empire.

Also: moth-eaten imitation camels

INSOLENT PORCUPINE

A large rodent covered in sharp spines, or quills, which are deployed in self-defence.

INVERTEBRATE

An animal without a backbone, or vertebral column. Examples include insects, arachnids, crustaceans and molluscs. An estimated 94 per cent of animal species are invertebrates. Haddock uses the term to berate a cowardly individual 'without a backbone'.

JACKANAPE

Describes an impudent, insolent and presumptuous man or mischievous child. Its use was first recorded in the fifteenth century as a nickname of William de la Pole, first Duke of Suffolk, whose badge was an ape's clog and chain. Later it was used as a name for someone who performed ape-like tricks.

JACKASS

An annoying dolt or blockhead; a male ass or donkey.

JACK-PUDDING

A clownish character or buffoon who appears in street performances and other public spectacles.

JELLIED EEL

A traditional English dish that originated in the eighteenth century in the East End of London, eels being plentiful in the River Thames. Chopped eels are boiled in a spiced stock. Because they are gelatinous, they release proteins that naturally turn the liquid into jelly. The dish is eaten cold.

JELLYFISH

A marine cnidarian with a dome-shaped body that is gelatinous and transparent. It has stinging tentacles hanging from the edge of its body to harpoon prey. The strange creatures of the deep are something of a fixation for the Captain when it comes to insults, particularly the invertebrates, which symbolise his hatred of cowardice.

Also: prize purple jellyfish

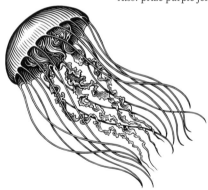

JOBBERNOWL

This archaic term refers to the head of a stupid or foolish person, particularly if it is misshapen.

JOKER

One who likes making jokes or joking around. In a pack of playing cards, the joker is the card that does not belong to any of the four suits.

JUDAS

Judas Iscariot was the disciple who betrayed Jesus to his enemies for 30 pieces of silver. Learning that Jesus was to be crucified as a result of his betrayal, Judas attempted to return the money he had been paid and, unable to do so, took his own life. The name has come to mean a traitor who betrays their friends or country.

KLEPTOMANIAC

Someone with a morbid tendency to steal. Kleptomaniacs have an irresistible urge to take things, even though they may not want or need them.

KOUA KOUAKOUIN KOUINKOUIN KOUA KOUIN KOUA

The Captain runs through a string of vowels, interspersed with 'k': the voiceless velar plosive, indicative of speechlessness. Uttered down the telephone at the arch-irritants Thomson and Thompson, this is one of the few occasions for which Haddock has no recourse to his extensive vocabulary.

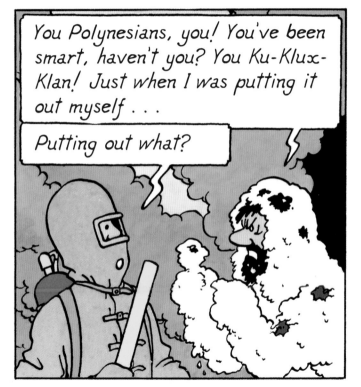

KU KLUX KLAN

The Ku Klux Klan, or KKK, is an American white supremacist hate group. Founded shortly after the American Civil War, its aims were to overthrow the state governments in the south and prevent the black population from exercising their right to vote. Klan members dressed in (often colourful) robes, masks and pointed hoods, designed both to intimidate and to conceal their identities. Banned in the 1870s, the KKK reappeared in 1915 in Atlanta, Georgia, reaffirming its racist, xenophobic, anti-Semitic and anti-Catholic views. By this time, the movement was funded by initiation fees and the sale of its distinctive now white uniform. This movement saw the emergence of cross-burnings. Membership of the Klan had declined significantly by the late 1920s. The third incarnation of the KKK emerged in the 1950s and 60s, working primarily to oppose the Civil Rights Movement. The group is still considered by the US government to be a terrorist organisation.

LANDLUBBERS

A person who knows nothing about the sea or sailing, having remained on land throughout their lives. It is a derogatory term deriving from the seventeenth century, although 'lubber' was used from the fourteenth century to describe a clumsy or stupid person.

Also: crew of landlubbers; lily-livered landlubbers; lubberly scum

LEPIDOPTERA

An order of insects characterised by scale-covered wings. The order is made up of butterflies and moths, and larvae that are caterpillars.

LOGARITHM

In mathematics, a logarithm is the power to which a given number must be raised in order to get to another

> Thundering typhoons! He's right! ... She's getting further away. Who's the bath-tub admiral commanding that crew of landlubbers?

> What now? How can we attract their attention?

given number. The fixity of a logarithmic system would not be attractive to Haddock, a free spirit in so many ways. The luckless policeman who is the target of his rage has already disappointed Haddock by offering him mineral water rather than something stronger; one wonders if Haddock would be as angry if the drink in question were Loch Lomond whisky.

LOON

A ridiculous, silly or outrageous person. The common loon is a bird with a haunting cry that was thought to resemble the howls of the insane.

LUNATIC

An antiquated term to describe someone who is mentally ill or dangerous.

MADHOUSE

A wild place that is full of confusion and noise, like hospitals for the mentally ill were commonly thought to be.

MAMELUKE

A mameluke, or mamluk, was a member of the military class, originally Turkish slave-soldiers, that ruled Egypt for three centuries from 1250 until 1517, when the country was conquered by the Ottomans under Sultan Selim I. The mamelukes remained powerful until the massacre of their leaders in 1811 by the Governor of Egypt, Muhammad Ali.

MEDDLESOME CABIN-BOY

From the seventeenth century onwards, boys as young as seven were employed as servants, or cabin-boys, for the officers and passengers on a ship. They had to clean, help the cook, carry food and messages, and go aloft to stow the sails. Some had to carry gunpowder from below decks to supply the gun crews manning the cannons on the upper deck.

MEGACYCLE

A unit of frequency equivalent to one million cycles per second. The term has been replaced by megahertz.

MEGALOMANIAC

A megalomaniac is someone who exhibits an excessive self-importance and self-regard. Megalomania is sometimes considered to be a mental illness, where the sufferer has delusions of power or grandeur. The Emperor Nero, Adolf Hitler and Marshal Kûrvi-Tasch, fascist ruler of Borduria, were all megalomaniacs.

MERINO LAMB

Merino is a breed of sheep that originated in Spain and is renowned for its long, fine wool.

MILEAGE-MERCHANT

An archaic term for roadside fuel vendors, here employed by Haddock as an indication of his contempt for over-reliance on the automobile. The Captain much prefers to travel on the high seas – his principle involvement with cars is to narrowly avoid being run over by them.

Also: infernal mileage-merchants

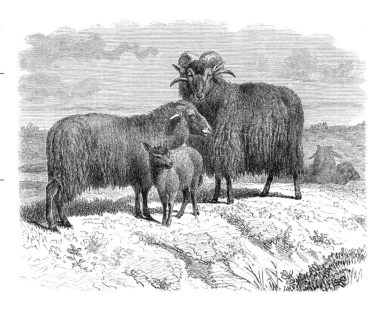

MILK-MAID

A woman or girl who milks cows or is employed in a dairy to make the butter and cheese.

MISERABLE

Unhappy, pitiful, worthy of pity.

Also: miserable bird;
miserable blundering barbecued blister;
miserable earth worms;
miserable iconoclast;
miserable miser;
miserable molecule of mildew;
miserable reptile;
miserable whipper-snapper

MISGUIDED MISSILE

A projectile without control; a body thrown carelessly. In contrast, Hergé very deliberately guides Haddock's cranium into that of General Alcazar in *The Red Sea Sharks*, setting in motion the events of the adventure. 'The [story] is too improbable,' opines the Captain, little realising that he himself is a 'guided missile'.

MISTER MULE

A mule is the offspring of a jack (male donkey) and a mare (female horse), usually sterile and used as a beast of burden. Mules are considered to be stubborn, sometimes refusing to budge, hence the phrase 'stubborn as a mule'.

MONKEY

A small to medium-sized primate, typically with a long tail. There are more than 250 species of monkey, found in North, Central and South America, Africa, Asia and Europe. The term also refers to a naughty or mischievous person, especially a child. Perhaps as a result of the encounter with the rifle-stealing monkeys in *Red Rackham's Treasure*, the first insult Haddock uses against his child-nemesis Abdullah is to compare him to an ape. Haddock's feelings for Abdullah are confused – one moment his eyes fill with tears at his childish antics, the next he is erupting at the effects of an exploding cigar. Abdullah's feelings for Haddock are clearly those of admiration; he is the first afficionado of Haddock's outbursts, christening him 'Blistering Barnacles'.

MONOPOLIZER

A person who monopolizes; often someone who amasses a commodity in large quantities in order to cause scarcity and then resell it at a higher price.

MONSTER

A large and frightening creature, conjured up in the imagination. Also describes a horribly cruel or savage person.

MORON

A foolish or stupid person.

Also: musical morons

MOTH-EATEN MARMOT

A heavily built, bushy tailed, burrowing rodent, the marmot lives in mountains in Europe, Asia and North America. This herbivore is also known as the ground squirrel.

Also: moth-eaten imitation camels

MOUJIK

A moujik, or muzhik, is a term for a Russian serf, an indentured labourer, usually rendered in English as 'peasant'. Haddock, reaching for a synonym for inferiority, is in no mood to consider the finer historical points of the persecution of the moujik by the Russian aristocracy.

MOUNTAINOUS MENAGERIE

A collection of wild or unusual animals or people.

MOUNTEBANK

Derived from the sixteenth-century Italian *montambanco* (from *monta in banco* meaning 'climb on the bench'), this is a charlatan or trickster, originally one selling quack medicine from a platform, or bench, in a public place.

Also: pithecanthropic mountebanks

MURDERER

A person who, deliberately and illegally, kills another human being.

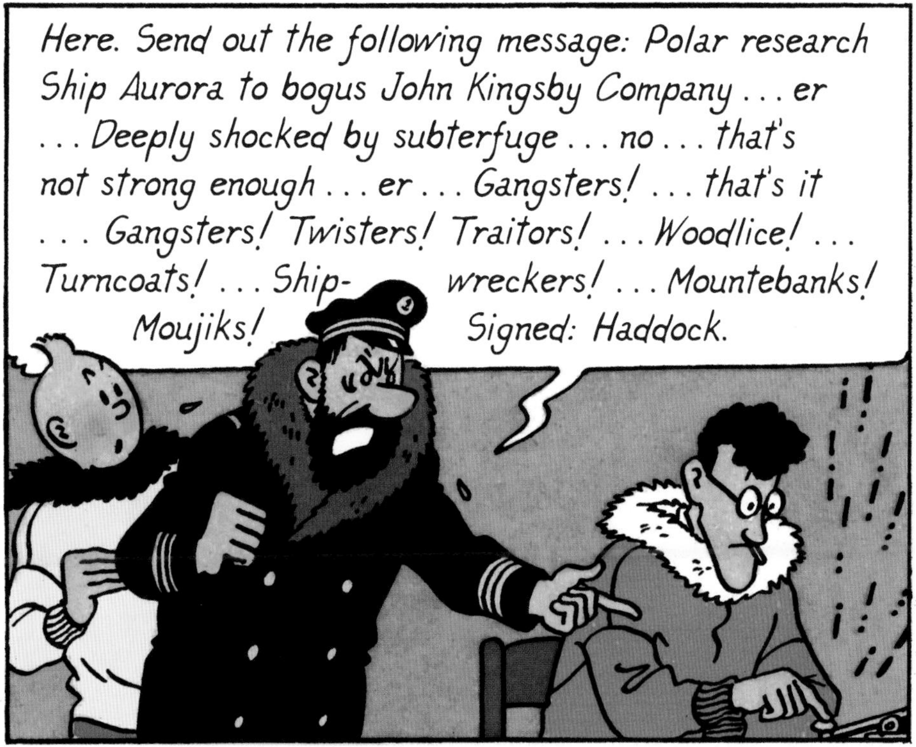
Here. Send out the following message: Polar research Ship Aurora to bogus John Kingsby Company . . . er . . . Deeply shocked by subterfuge . . . no . . . that's not strong enough . . . er . . . Gangsters! . . . that's it . . . Gangsters! Twisters! Traitors! . . . Woodlice! . . . Turncoats! . . . Ship-wreckers! . . . Mountebanks! Moujiks! Signed: Haddock.

NANNY-GOAT

A female goat.

Also: goat

NINCOMPOOP

A simpleton; someone who is silly or stupid.

Also: prize nincompoop

NITWIT

A slow-witted, foolish or scatter-brained person. The insults used by Haddock to abuse those he considers to be of low intelligence are numerous. The slang term nitwit is an American import, deriving from 'nit', meaning 'nothing' in dialectal German or Yiddish, and the Old English 'wit' meaning 'mental capacity', 'sense' or 'understanding'.

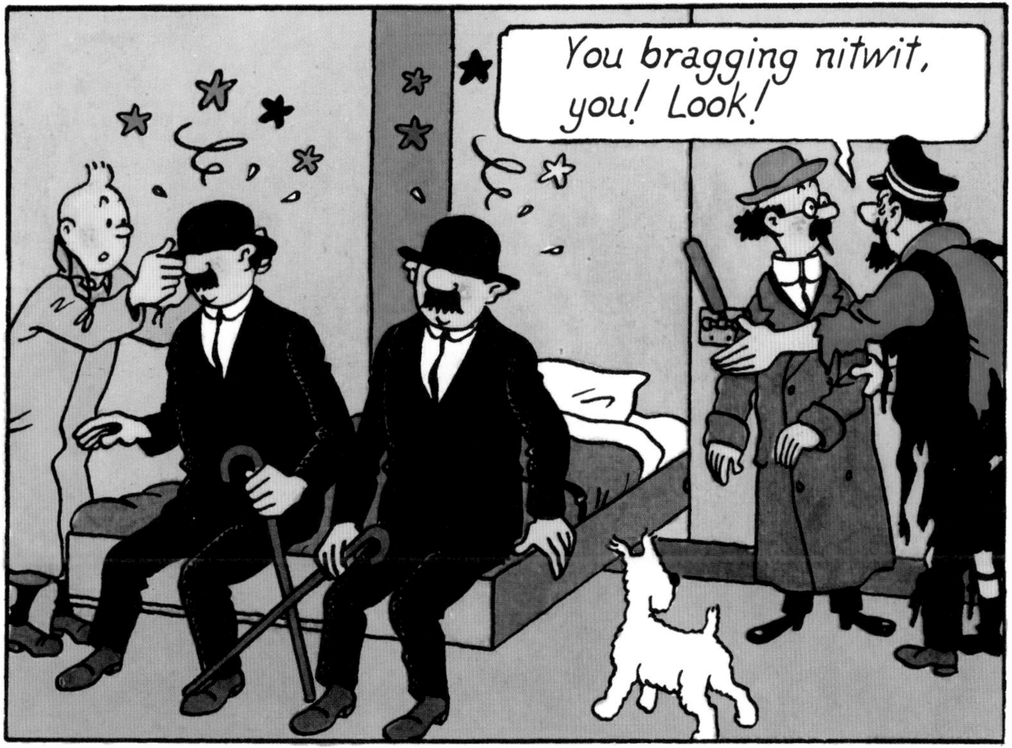
You bragging nitwit, you! Look!

NIT-WITTED NINE-PIN

A ninepin is a wooden skittle used in the traditional bowling game called Ninepins, played in an alley. The object of the game is to knock down as many of the nine wooden skittles as possible with each roll of a wooden ball.

Also: nitwitted numbskull; thundering nitwitted numbskull; thundering nitwitted sea-gherkin

NUMBSKULL

Someone with a muddled head; a dunce.

NYCTALOP

Someone afflicted by nyctalopia, the inability to see normally in dim light or 'night blindness'. At the moment this leaps into Haddock's mind, the sun has just come out after a prolonged period of rain – possibly affecting the vision of the nyctalopic truck driver, who soaks Haddock to the bone by driving through a puddle.

OAF

Someone who is clumsy and lacking in intelligence.

Also: clumsy oaf

ODD-TOED UNGULATE

A hoofed mammal. Some ungulates are perissodactyls (odd-toed), such as horses, rhinoceroses and tapirs, and some are artiodactyls (even-toed), such as cattle, sheep and hippopotamuses.

OLYMPIC ATHLETE

A person who competes in the Olympic Games, which originated in ancient Greece 3,000 years ago. The games were revived in the late nineteenth century and have become the most important sports events in the modern world. The first modern games took place in Athens, and featured 280 athletes from 13 nations competing in 43 events. In the 2016 Summer Olympics, held in Rio, 11,238 athletes from 207 nations took part in 306 events.

OPHICLEIDE

An early brass instrument belonging to the bugle family, with a long tube, doubling back on itself, and keys for fingering. It was replaced by the tuba in orchestral music at the end of the nineteenth century.

ORANGUTANG

This endangered 'man of the forest' (its name in Malay) lives a solitary life in the forests of Borneo and Sumatra. The orangutang is a large, long-armed ape with shaggy, red fur. It is the largest arboreal mammal and spends most of its time in the trees.

OSTROGOTH

The Ostrogoths, or East Goths, were a branch of a Germanic tribe, the Goths, that rose to prominence during the late Roman Empire. The Ostrogoths developed an empire north of the Black Sea in the third century, before invading Italy in the fifth century and founding a Gothic kingdom there, under Theodoric the Great. The kingdom survived until its invasion by Byzantine emperor Justinian I in 535. By extension, an Ostrogoth is a 'barbarian' with a disregard for order and decorum.

Also: Visigoth

PACHYRHIZUS

A genus of five or six species of tropical and subtropical plants with edible tuberous roots, among which is the Mexican yam. The sweet, juicy root can be eaten raw or cooked. Haddock reserves this obscure but characterful epithet for the vain and egotistical General Tapioca in *Tintin and the Picaros*.

PAIR OF PERAMBULATING FIRE-PUMPS

A fire-pump is part of a fire protection system's water supply, found on a fire-fighting vehicle or in a sprinkler system. It is a fitting metaphor for the llama, a ruminant mammal from the Andes mountains, which, Haddock discovers, can unleash a large quantity of spittle with considerable force.

PARANOIAC

This is another word for 'paranoid', which describes someone who is extremely suspicious and afraid of other people or perceived events without any grounds to be so.

PARASITE

A small plant or animal that lives on or inside a larger plant or animal, its 'host', upon which it feeds. Scabies, head lice, tapeworms or *Phylloxera* are types of parasite. Figuratively, the term refers to a person who takes from others without giving back, or who lives in idleness at the expense of society. Jolyon Wagg might be considered a parasite when he settled in Moulinsart with his whole family.

Also: Phylloxera

PATAGONIAN

Patagonia is a dry, grassy region in southern South America, east of the Andes, including the southernmost parts of Argentina and Chile; the Boundary Treaty of 1881 established the division of this vast region between the two countries. The indigenous peoples of Patagonia, also referred to as the Tehuelche, encompassed a number of separate groups with their own unique dialects and traditions. The influx of European settlers led to the swift decline, and eventual extinction, of these native tribespeople.

Also: Patagonian pirates; Patagonian savages

PCHKRAAPRVT

There are times when even the most eloquent are lost for words!

PEST

An insect or small animal that damages crops, livestock or humans. In Haddock's case, the list of 'pests' is long, including, but not limited to: insects, animals, Jolyon Wagg, Thomson and Thompson, the weather, deafness, gossip magazines, Bianca Castafiore and her entourage, careless drivers, children, people who dial the wrong number, and anyone who dares interpose themself between the Captain and a glass or three of Loch Lomond.

Also: man-eating pests; pestilential parakeet; pestilential pachyderm

PHYLLOXERA

A type of insect of the genus *Phylloxera* that typically feeds on plant juices, particularly those of the grapevine. The aphid *Phylloxera vastatrix* attacks the roots of the grapevine, feeding on its sap. In the nineteenth century, disease caused by this tiny insect spread through wine-producing regions of France with disastrous effect; an estimated half of all vineyards were affected. The parasite remains a ever-present threat to winegrowers, and for Haddock, one of the most serious scourges known to humankind.

PICAROON

Rogues, vagabonds, thieves or brigands. Also used to describe someone who acts as a pirate.

PICKLED HERRING

A traditional way of preserving herring, a popular food in many parts of Europe. The fish is cured with salt, which extracts water, then the herring is soaked in a brine made from vinegar, salt and sugar. Pickled herring is one of the twelve dishes traditionally served on Christmas Eve in Russia, Poland, Lithuania and the Ukraine.

Billions of blue blistering barnacles! Pirates! They'll need a distress signal when I get hold of them!

PIRATE

An adventurer who sails the seas pillaging ships. Figuratively speaking, a person who gets rich at the expense of others.

Also: interplanetary pirate; Patagonian pirates

PITHECANTHROPUS

An intermediate primate between a common ape ancestor and *Homo sapiens*. The visionary sailor, Sir Francis Haddock, used this word in 1698 to insult the notorious pirate Red Rackham, approximately 170 years ahead of its generally accepted coinage by the German zoologist Ernst Haeckel . . . or perhaps the Captain's identification with his illustrious ancestor overcomes him!

Also: pithecanthropic mountebanks; pithecanthropic pickpocket; pithecanthropic pock-mark

POCK-MARK

A small mark or scar on the skin, usually permanent, caused by smallpox or acne. Smallpox, commonly known as 'pox', was effectively eradicated through vaccination by 1979.

Also: pockmarked pin-headed pirate of a pilot

POLITICIAN

A person professionally involved in politics, especially a member of a government who may have been elected to the position. Also used to describe a person who is good at using situations to gain advancement or advantage. The vacillations and equivocations of the political class are naturally an anathema to the Captain, whose no-nonsense approach to life is entirely at odds with such fripperies.

POLTROON

A man without courage or honour.

POLYGRAPH

An early device for reproducing writings or drawings, derived from the Greek *polugraphos*, meaning 'writing copiously'. A somewhat obscure insult from Haddock, aimed as it is, at a speeding vehicle.

POLYNESIAN

Natives or inhabitants of the islands that make up the area called Polynesia in the Pacific ocean, extending from Hawaii in the north, to Easter Island in the east and New Zealand in the west. The main groups of Polynesian islands include the Cook Islands, French Polynesia, Samoa, Tonga and Tuvalu.

PRATTLING PORPOISE

Porpoises are small cetacean mammals of the genus *Phocaena*.

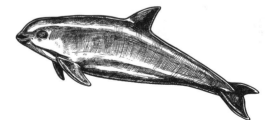

PROFITEER

A trader who makes large profits by charging exorbitantly high prices for goods that are hard to get. The entrepreneur Laszlo Carreidas is one such unscrupulous individual, contemptible in the eyes of Haddock who despises exploitation of any kind.

PSYCHOPATH

A person who is amoral, antisocial and unable to establish meaningful personal relationships. Psychopathy is a severe form of antisocial personality disorder, whereby an individual may be impulsive, irresponsible, behave violently towards other people, and feel no regret for doing so. Criminal behaviour is a key feature of antisocial personality disorder. It is not known why some people develop antisocial personality disorders, but genetics and traumatic childhood experiences are thought to play a role. Psychopath and sociopath are often used interchangeably in common parlance.

PYROGRAPHER

An artist who burns designs onto a surface, such as wood or leather, with a heated tool. It is also known as pokerwork.

PYROMANIAC

One who is driven by an irresistible compulsion to set things on fire. Pyromania is distinct from arson; an arsonist sets fires in a deliberate and calculating manner, for personal, monetary or political gain.

PUFFED-UP PUNCHINELLO

Punchinella was a fat, humpbacked male puppet or marionette in Italian puppet shows of *commedia dell'arte* in the seventeenth century. Originating in Naples, the puppet was then taken by showmen all over Europe, becoming Polichinelle in France and Purchinelas in Spain. The tradition arrived in England after the restoration of Charles II in 1660, where the name was shortened to Punch, first appearing in the writings of the diarist Samuel Pepys in 1662. By 1700, most puppet shows in England featured Punch and his wife Judy.

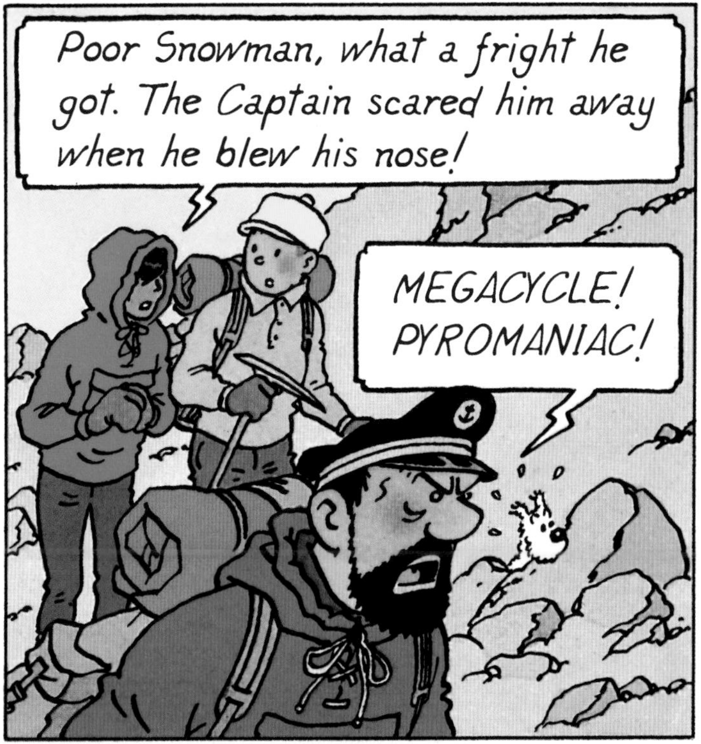
Poor Snowman, what a fright he got. The Captain scared him away when he blew his nose!
MEGACYCLE! PYROMANIAC!

R

RAGGLE-TAGGLE RUMINANT

A motley crew, or odd mixture of artiodactyl mammals, which ruminate or chew the cud, bringing back food from their stomach to chew again. The group includes deer, antelopes, cattle, sheep, bison, goats, giraffes and camels.

RAPSCALLION

The archaic form of 'rascallion', meaning a rogue or a scamp. In the seventeenth century, the term was used commonly to mean rascal or vagabond.

RASCAL

A dishonest, unscrupulous or mischievous person – one of the rabble.

RAT

A long-tailed rodent, found all over the world. Thanks to their astonishing reproductive capacity and proclivity to devour anything, rats are extremely destructive pests, as well as carriers of contagious diseases, such as bubonic plague and typhus. The term is used, by Haddock and more generally, to refer to a sneaky or untrustworthy individual.

RATTLESNAKE

A type of pit viper that has a series of interlocking pieces of keratin that click together to form the tip of its tail. Special muscles vibrate the tail at up to 90 times a second, making the keratin pieces knock together to produce the threatening 'rattle'.

Also: snake; viper

REPROBATE

An unprincipled and disreputable person with no morals.

RHIZOPOD

A protozoa of the phylum Rhizopoda, a group that includes the amoebas and foraminifera. These tiny creatures use a temporary protrusion called a pseudopod ('false foot') to move around.

RKRPXZKRMTFRZ

See PCHKRAAPRVT.

ROAD HOG

A clumsy, uncourteous, or even dangerous driver.

ROAD ROLLER

A vehicle that is used to compact and roll flat soil, gravel or asphalt when roads or other flat surfaces are being built.

RUBBER-NECK

A term referring to people who turn to look or stare when passing unusual events or disasters, such as road accidents, craning their necks to see what is happening.

RUFFIAN

A hoodlum or lawless person; someone who acts violently in a criminal way.

SAN THEODOLITE

This is Haddock's malapropism for San Theodorians, the citizens of the South American country of San Theodoros. A theodolite is a measuring instrument used to measure angles while surveying land. The Haddockism also bears a hint of the paleontological terms used extensively by the Captain to suggest underdevelopment, for example Cro-Magnon or belemnite.

SAVAGE

A highly derogatory term to refer to a member of a primitive society or, more commonly, a crude or uncivilised person. The Captain has occasionally used the term in a misleading way, for example to describe the Incas, a highly advanced civilisation.

Also: ill-mannered savages

SCALLYWAG

A scamp or rascal.

SCARECROW

An object, often in the shape of a human, placed in a garden or field of crops to scare away the birds that might otherwise cause damage. Colloquially the term refers to an untidy-looking person, or something that looks dangerous but is in actual fact harmless. It is one of numerous insults hurled by the Captain at the Yeti, the supposed thief of his whisky, in *Tintin in Tibet*.

SCORPION

An arachnid of the order Scorpionida, found in warm, dry regions of the world. Scorpions have a segmented body with a long tail, at the end of which is a venomous, and deadly, sting. By extension, 'scorpion' refers to someone who exhibits malevolence. Captain Haddock's corrupt ex-shipmate, Allan, now a mercenary, is the deserved recipient of this stinging epithet in *Flight 714 to Sydney*.

SCUM

An offensive term used to describe people who are so low or disgusting that they are not worth considering.

Also: lubberly scum

SEA-GHERKIN

A species of sea cucumber in the family *Cucumariidae*. This long-bodied echinoderm lives on the floor of the Atlantic ocean and the Mediterranean sea and scavenges for small organisms with the branched and retractile tentacles round its mouth. 'Ceci n'est pas une pipe,' wrote another famous Belgian artist, Magritte. The sea-gherkin resembles a gherkin, but is not related to it. When one thing pretends to be another, Haddock's straightforward instincts cannot resist drawing attention to the inauthentic.

Also: sea-lice; sea-serpent; sea-trout; thundering nitwitted sea-gherkins

SEALION

This eared seal belongs to the family *Otariidae*. It is found in most of the world's oceans, spending up to two years at sea at a time before returning to land to breed in large colonies on rocks and sandy shores.

SECOND-RATE SON OF A SWORD-SWALLOWER

Sword-swallowing is a dangerous ancient art that originated in India more than 4,000 years ago. Learning to do it safely can take years. Performers pass a sword through their mouth and oesophagus to their stomach, and need to relax their throats enough for the blade to slide down smoothly without doing serious damage.

Also: son of a sea-gherkin; son of a sea-serpent

SHIPWRECKER

A person who causes shipwrecks by lighting misleading signals along the coast, causing ships to run aground. Wreckers made a living from plundering wrecked ships, sometimes killing any sailors who survived. One can imagine that Haddock took a dim view of this practice.

SIAMESE TWINS

An out-dated name for conjoined twins.

SLAVE TRADER

Someone who traffics slaves – in Haddock's mind, the greatest possible abomination and a heinous departure from the values of the Merchant Navy. Haddock's encounter with a slave trader in *The Red Sea Sharks* gives rise to the lengthiest, and most vehement, torrent of abuse launched at any single character in the whole of his adventures – deservedly so.

SLUBBERDEGUL-LION

A filthy, slobbering or slovenly person, not worth bothering with.

SLUGGARD

A habitually slow and lazy person.

Also: boneidle builder

SNAKE

A reptile without feet. The snake has inspired disgust and revulsion since ancient times. It is the snake, or serpent, that tempts Eve in the book of Genesis. 'Snake' has become synonymous with a treacherous or a hypocritical individual, and Haddock makes frequent use of the term and its variants.

Also: rattlesnake; serpent; viper

SPARROW

A small brown and grey bird of the *Passeridae* family, with a stout body, rounded wings and conical beak, adapted for eating seeds.

SPITFIRE

A person that has a fiery temper, is easily provoked and given to outbursts. Also a British single-engine fighter plane that became famous during World War II.

SQUAWKING POPINJAY

A popinjay is a parrot used as a target in archery and shooting; a woodpecker. Also a foppish, conceited person, given to vain displays and empty chatter.

STEAMING BLOOD

One of the Captain's more unpleasantly visceral insults, this gory image speaks for itself.

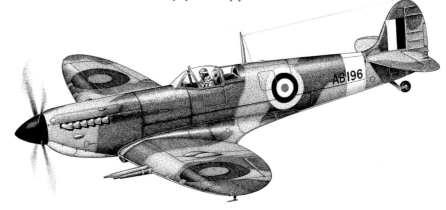

STEAM-ROLLER

A heavy vehicle used to crush, compact and level roads or building materials. In the past, the vehicle was powered by steam. The term also refers to a person who forces others to bend to their will or ignores what they have to say, steam-rollering over them.

STOOL-PIGEON

A spy or informer, particularly for the police; a nark. Also a dummy used to decoy others. The stool-pigeon was said to originate from the practice of tying a pigeon to a stool. In its struggles, the pigeon would attract other birds that could be easily killed. In addressing the unconscionable slave trader in *The Red Sea Sharks* with this epithet, Haddock reveals his contempt for people who betray others for their own gain.

SUBTROPICAL SEA-LOUSE

A sea-louse is a parasite found on marine fish worldwide, especially in warm and tropical waters. They eat fish mucus, skin and blood but do not harm humans.

SWINE

A pig or herd of pigs. Used as an insult against someone thought to be malicious, particularly if they have been unpleasant towards you.

Also: cunning swine

SYCOPHANT

A self-seeking, fawning person, who thinks that servile flattery will induce powerful people to favour them.

TECHNOCRAT

A scientist, engineer or other expert who exerts political power as well as technical knowledge, and who favours science as a organising principle, possibly at the expense of human factors.

TEDDY-BEAR

A child's stuffed, furry toy, named after Teddy (Theodore) Roosevelt, twenty-sixth president of the USA, from 1901 to 1909. Also someone who acts big and tough, but at heart is a lovable, soft, endearing person. Haddock's intuition in using this epithet for the Yeti in *Tintin in Tibet* proves correct – it turns out that the Yeti is less abominable that one might assume. In belittling the creature, Haddock also hopes to make it seem less imposing.

TERRAPIN

A small, thick-shelled turtle that lives partly in fresh or brackish water and partly on land. These reptiles feed on small aquatic animals.

TERRORIST

A proponent of terrorism, a practice founded on violence and terror.

THUG

A brutal, vicious person or criminal.

Also: trigger-happy thug

THUNDERING TYPHOON

A typhoon is a type of cyclone that forms in the northwestern Pacific ccean due to the specific climactic conditions found there. The use of 'thundering typhoons' (and its many variants) as an expletive is an indication of the importance of meteorological conditions to the sailor. As a well-travelled seaman, it is likely that Haddock would have sailed through such storms, and would have personal experience of their devastating effects. In *The Seven Crystal Balls*, the Captain mentions having sailed through a hurricane 'many years ago', so it is possible that he has also navigated a typhoon in his travels.

Uttered in *The Red Sea Sharks,* the masterful 'Billions of bilious blue blistering barnacles in a thundering typhoon' is notable for being the Captain's longest curse.

Also: blue blistering barnacles in
   a thundering typhoon;
billions of blue blistering
   barnacles in a thundering typhoon;
licorice-livered lubberly scum in
   thousands of thundering typhoons
ten thousand thundering typhoons;
thousands of thundering typhoons

TIN-CAN CONTRAPTION

A machine or mode of transport that is flimsy and does not work well.

TIN-HATTED TYRANT

A person in authority who has complete power and wields it oppressively in a cruel and unfair way is said to be a tyrant. Aimed squarely at a metal-hat-wearing Inca priest, Haddock is here revelling in an iconoclasm of his own.

TOAD

A contemptible person, the object of disgust or aversion. Also a tail-less amphibian, a close relative of frogs in the family *Bufonidae*, the toad has dry, warty skin and spends less time in the water.

TOFFEE-NOSE

To be toffee-nosed is to behave with an unwarranted superior manner. The term is said to derive from the word 'toff', used to describe an upper-class Englishman, and the habit that such a person may have of looking down their nose at those they consider inferior.

TORTURER

A person who deliberately inflicts severe physical or mental pain on someone in order to punish them, get a confession or information, or simply because they are cruel.

TRAFFICKER IN HUMAN FLESH

A slaver trader; the most contemptible way imaginable in which to make a profit.

TRAMP

A homeless vagrant who wanders from place to place, either earning money with casual work or begging.

Also: saucy tramp

TROGLODYTE

A cave dweller. The earliest references to trogodytes are from the Greco-Roman period. The historian Herodotus described them as swift runners, who ate snakes and made guttural cries like the screeching of bats. Colloquially, the term is used to describe an unsophisticated individual.

Also: two-timing troglodytes

TURNCOAT

A disloyal person who changes their allegiance to a person, organisation or regime.

TWISTER

A cheat or rogue who twists the truth.

Also: two-timing Tartar twister

TWO-FACED TRAITOR

A person guilty of treachery or betrayal. Loyalty is a defining feature of our hero, and he freely reins insult upon those he considers to be traitors. To hide a betrayal is to compound its gravity; Haddock cannot bear a hypocrite.

TWOPENNY-HALFPENNY COASTGUARDS

Ineffectual or half-hearted coastal surveillance, such as might fail to thwart the activity of a pirate.

VAGABOND

A homeless person who is nomadic, travelling from place to place; a drifter. The term is generally used, including by Haddock, in a derogatory sense, implying someone disreputable and lacking a sense of responsibility.

VAMPIRE

A vampire is a corpse that emerges from its grave at night to drink the blood of the living. As such, vampires are among the 'living dead' or 'undead' who continue to exist as living beings, with consciousness, movement and speech, while being biologically dead. Vampires have featured in folklore, mostly European, for hundreds of years, and have become part of popular culture. To survive, a vampire needs fresh blood, preferably human, which it usually drinks from the neck of its victim. A vampire's bite has the power to

reanimate a corpse as a vampire. Further supernatural powers include the ability to transform into a bat or wolf, mind-control and shapeshifting. Vampires reside in their original grave or coffin, which must, according to many traditions, contain their native soil. Further characteristics include a strong aversion to garlic (one clove of which is enough to drive them away), sunlight, religious symbols such as the crucifix and holy water, which will afflict burns. It is said that a vampire casts no shadow and has no reflection. The surest way to kill one is to drive a wooden stake through its heart.

The most famous vampire is Count Dracula, introduced in Bram Stoker's 1897 novel *Dracula*, which is set between England and Transylvania (not to be confused with Trans-Syldavia, the eastern province of the kingdom of Syldavia).

In common parlance, a vampire is a person who preys ruthlessly upon others, such as a blackmailer.

VANDAL

A member of an East Germanic tribe, renowned for its wanton destruction. The Vandals famously sacked Rome in 455, plundering the city for fourteen days. They battled the Huns and the Goths, and founded a kingdom in North Africa that later fell to Byzantine forces and was assimilated into the Byzantine empire. Also, a person who deliberately causes damage or destruction to personal or public property.

VEGETARIAN

Someone who excludes meat and fish from their diet. Forced to become vegetarian by Snowy in *The Shooting Star*, Haddock remains bitter about the experience.

VERMICELLI

Meaning 'little worms' in Italian, vermicelli are fine, spaghetti-like strands of pasta, often used in soup.

VIPER

A venomous snake from the *Viperidae* family. Despite the fear they engender, vipers must be given credit for their contribution to agriculture, as they feed on rodents that would otherwise threaten crops.

Figuratively speaking, the term refers to a malicious, spiteful or treacherous person.

VISIGOTH

A member of a division of the Goths. The Visigoths separated from the Ostrogoths in the fourth century and went on to establish kingdoms in Gaul and Spain. The tribe was renowned for its brutality, and Haddock uses the term to imply brutishness, rudeness and lack of culture.

Also: Ostrogoth

VIVISECTIONIST

A person who operates on living organisms for experimental purposes. Also a person who advocates the practice of vivisection as being necessary for the advancement of science. Greek physicians Herophilus and Erasistratus are thought to be the first to systematically perform vivisection, including on criminals. The practice was then, and remains now, highly controversial. The use of vivisection on animals was pioneered by Galen of Pergamon, another Greek physician (vivisections on humans being strictly prohibited at the time). Might we deduce that Haddock, out of affection for Snowy, is a committed anti-vivisectionist?

VULTURE

A large bird of prey of the family *Accipitridae* that scavenges on carrion, in other words, dead and putrefying flesh. It is used as a term of abuse to describe a person who preys on someone else in order to profit from their problems.

WEEVIL

One of the beetles that belong to the family *Culculionidae*. A weevil has a hard shell and a very long snout. It feeds on grains and seeds and is considered a pest because it often destroy crops. Jolyon Wagg, the insurance salesman whose self-importance and lack of self-awareness infuriates Haddock, is the unlucky recipient of this, and many other, epithets.

D'you imagine for one moment that I'd let a young whippersnapper like you go off alone? Not on your life! I suppose you think that Captain Haddock has got tomato juice in his veins, eh?

But you . . .

WHIPPERSNAPPER

Someone who is behaving more confidently than they have the right to – particularly applied to a young, cheeky person. Once in a blue moon, the Captain's frustrations with Tintin's precociousness overboil. The origins of 'whippersnapper' are from a seventeenth century term for an idle youngster with nothing better to do than crack a whip to while away their time. Haddock is clearly misguided here – no one could be more industrious than the hard-working Tintin.

WILDCAT

The wildcat, or *Felis silvestris*, is a small cat that is found in many different countries and is impossible to tame. Domesticated cats are descended from the African sub-species. A person who is violent or easily angered is often described as a wildcat.

WOLF IN SHEEP'S CLOTHING

A malicious person out to do harm but who presents themselves as a friendly, helpful person.

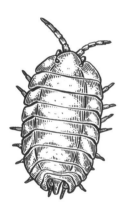

WOODLOUSE

This crustacean is a hardy minibeast with a flattened, elliptical body and built-in armour. It likes to hide in warm, moist places such as compost heaps. Some roll into balls if they are threatened so their armour can protect them better.

WRETCH

Someone who is so unfortunate and unhappy that you feel sympathy for them. The phrase can be used to describe an unpleasant, annoying or wicked person.

Also: miserable wretch

ZAPOTEC

A member of an indigenous people living in the Valley of Oaxaca in Mexico (not be confused with Emil Zátopek, the triple-gold-medal-winning Czechoslovakian long-distance runner). The Zapotecan civilisation originated in the late sixth century BCE and flourished until the arrival of the Spanish conquistadors in 1522. The indigenous Zapotecs living in and around Oaxaca today call themselves Ben 'Zaa, or 'Cloud People'. A number of ancient beliefs and practices still survive, including the custom that the dead should be buried with their possessions for use in the afterlife.

Also: thundering herd of Zapotecs

ZOMBIE

In the voodoo religion of west Africa and Haiti, zombies are people revived with 'zombie powders' by a practitioner called a bokor. In the popular culture of science fiction and horror in book and film, a zombie is an undead creature with a re-animated body that can destroy the living, changing some people they attack into zombies themselves.

Also: jolly zombies

... Deeply shocked by sub... not strong enough ... er ... ... Gangsters! Twisters! Turncoats! ... Shi... Moujiks!